TAMAR'S SUKKAH

This
PJ BOOK
belongs to

_____

_____

PJ Library®

JEWISH BEDTIME STORIES and SONGS

For Eema, who believes that children know a lot. — E.B.G.

To all children who love the adventures they find in their
own backyard — K.J.K.

Text copyright © 2015 by Ellie B. Gellman
Illustrations copyright © 2013 by Katherine Janus Kahn
All rights reserved. International copyright secured. No part of this book may be reproduced, stored in
a retrieval system, or transmitted in any form or by any means—electronic, mechanical, photocopying,
recording, or otherwise—without the prior written permission of Lerner Publishing Group, Inc., except
for the inclusion of brief quotations in an acknowledged review.

KAR-BEN PUBLISHING
A division of Lerner Publishing Group, Inc.
241 First Avenue North
Minneapolis, MN 55401 USA
1-800-4-KARBEN

Website address: www.karben.com

Main body text set in Chauncy Decaf 18/24.
Typeface provided by Chank.

Library of Congress Cataloging-in-Publication Data

Gellman, Ellie
    Tamar's sukkah / by Ellie B. Gellman ; illustrated by Katherine Janus Kahn.
        pages   cm.
    Summary: "Tamar and her friends, each one a little bigger and older, join to decorate a sukkah that is
just right"—Provided by publisher.
    ISBN: 978–1–4677–5636–5 (lib. bdg. : alk. paper)
    [1. Sukkah—Fiction. 2. Sukkot—Fiction. 3. Friendship—Fiction.] I. Kahn, Katherine, illustrator. II. Title.
PZ7.G2835Tam 2015
    [E]—dc23   2014029062

Manufactured in Hong Kong
1 – PN – 5/1/15

091515K1/B0731/A3

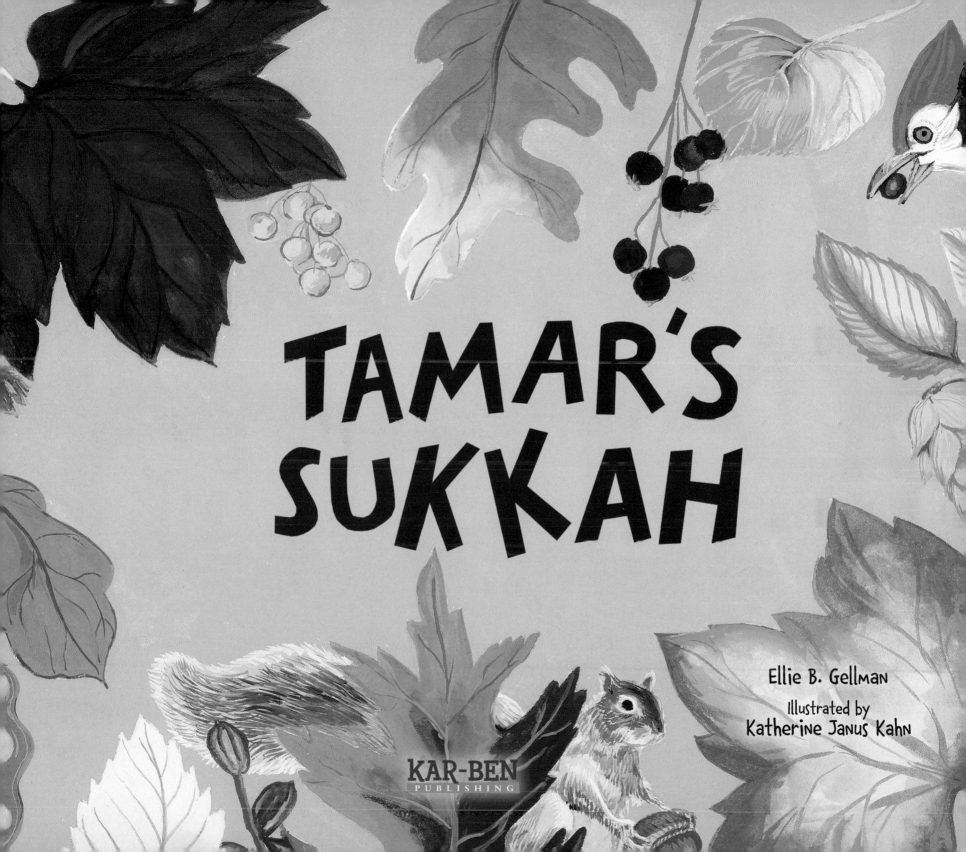

TAMAR'S SUKKAH

Ellie B. Gellman

Illustrated by
Katherine Janus Kahn

KAR-BEN
PUBLISHING

Tamar looked at the sukkah in her backyard. She had helped to build it just that morning, and she was very proud of it.

Still, something wasn't quite right. Something was missing.

It wasn't the walls. They were made of beautiful
brown cloth and seemed to reach the sky.

It wasn't the branches on the roof. They were leafy and green and gave the sukkah a wonderful smell.

Tamar thought for a minute. "I know what's missing," she said. She ran inside to
find paper and crayons. Carefully she drew round apples and colored them red.
Then she cut them out and tied a green loop of ribbon to each one.

But when she tried to hang the apples in the sukkah, she couldn't reach high enough. She was just too little. She would have to get help.

Danny lived next door. He was seven.

He could reach high enough
to hang the apples.

Danny took out a chair and climbed on top of it. He stretched as high as he could, and soon all the bright red apples swung above his head. "Perfect," said Danny.

"It looks nice," said Tamar. "But the sukkah still isn't quite right. Something is missing."

Danny thought for a minute. "I know what's missing," he said. He ran home.

A few minutes later he came back with a piece of posterboard and a box of markers. He drew a brown sukkah with red apples hanging from it and leafy branches on top. Then he took out the green marker and started to write in Hebrew.

"Baruch Atah . . . ," he wrote. Then he stopped. He wanted to put a blessing on his poster, the one to say when you sit in the sukkah, but he couldn't remember what came after the "Baruch" part. He would have to get help.

Shelly lived across the street.
She was nine.

She would know how to write the blessing.

Shelly took the marker and copied the blessing from a prayerbook. "It means 'thank you, God, for this happy holiday when we sit in the sukkah,'" said Shelly. She and Danny hung the poster on the sukkah wall.

"Beautiful!" said Shelly. "Perfect!" said Danny.

"It looks nice," said Tamar. "But the sukkah still isn't quite right. Something is missing." Shelly thought for a minute. "I know what's missing," she said, and ran home.

She came back a few minutes later with a white tablecloth. "This sukkah needs a table," she explained. "Here's the tablecloth, but I couldn't carry the table up from the basement. I need help."

Ari lived down the block.
He was eleven. He was strong enough to
carry the table. Ari and Shelly lifted and
pulled and carried the table up the basement
stairs and across the street.

בָּרוּךְ אַתָּה יְיָ
אֱלֹהֵינוּ מֶלֶךְ הָעוֹלָם
אֲשֶׁר קִדְּשָׁנוּ בְּמִצְוֺתָיו
וְצִוָּנוּ לֵישֵׁב בַּסֻּכָּה

Danny and Tamar brought chairs. When they got the table set up,
with the white cloth spread on it, they were very pleased.

"Great!" said Ari. "Beautiful!" said Shelly. "Perfect!" said Danny.

"It looks nice," said Tamar. "But the sukkah still isn't quite right. Something is missing."

Ari thought for a minute. "I know what's missing," he said. He ran home and came back a few minutes later with a bag of pretzels and a bottle of apple juice. "A sukkah is much more fun if we eat inside it," he explained.

"But we didn't have any paper cups at home. Maybe Rachel can help. She lives next to the drugstore. She can buy some cups and bring them to the sukkah. Let's call her."

Rachel rode up on her bike
a few minutes later, with a
package of cups. She poured
the juice carefully.

Soon everyone was busy munching pretzels and drinking apple juice.

"Fantastic!" said Rachel. "Great!" said Ari.
"Beautiful!" said Shelly. "Perfect!" said Danny.

"It's terrific!" said Tamar. "Now I think the sukkah is just right. Nothing is missing. It has walls and a roof, branches and decorations, a table and chairs, snacks and juice . . . and friends."

"A sukkah full of friends is just right."

"It is exactly what a sukkah should be."

Sukkot is a fall harvest holiday recalling the time when the Israelites wandered in the desert and lived in temporary huts. Many synagogues and Jewish families build harvest booths decorated with branches and fruit, and share festival meals there during the week-long holiday.

Ellie B. Gellman grew up in Minneapolis, where she first began telling stories to the children in her synagogue. She has taught in Jewish schools in the United States, Canada and Israel. Her previous books include *Netta and her Plant*, *Shai's Shabbat Walk* and *Jeremy's Dreidel*.

Katherine Janus Kahn, an illustrator, calligrapher, and sculptor, studied Fine Arts at the Bezalel School in Jerusalem and at the University of Iowa. She has illustrated many children's books including Kar-Ben's popular "Sammy Spider" series, a set of Family Services for Shabbat and the holidays, and many other award-winning books for young children. She lives in Wheaton, Maryland.